A Perfect Thanksgiving

By Sierra Harimann
Illustrated by The Artifact Group

SCHOLASTIC INC.

No part of this publication may be reproduced, stored in a retrieval system, or transmitted in any form or by any means, electronic, mechanical, photocopying, recording, or otherwise, without written permission of the publisher. For information regarding permission, write to Scholastic Inc., Attention: Permissions Department, 557 Broadway, New York, NY 10012.

ISBN 978-0-545-47232-6

© 2012 MEG. All Rights Reserved.

PUPPY IN MY POCKET® and all related titles, logos, and characters are registered trademarks of MEG. Licensed by Licensing Works!®

Published by Scholastic Inc. SCHOLASTIC and associated logos are trademarks and/or registered trademarks of Scholastic Inc. Lexile® is a registered trademark of MetaMetrics, Inc.

12 11 10 9 8 7 6 5 4 3 2 1   12 13 14 15 16 17/0

Designed by Angela Jun
Printed in the U.S.A.   40
First printing, September 2012

The air in Puppyville was cool and clear as Ivy, Montana, and Clarissa headed to the Hot Diggity Dog Market one Saturday morning.

"*Brrr*," Montana shivered as she pulled her hat down over her ears. "It's getting so cold!"

"I know, but I love this weather!" Ivy barked. "My favorite holiday is in the fall—Thanksgiving!"

"*Mmmm*, Thanksgiving," Clarissa agreed. "I love stuffing and mashed potatoes."

"Well, you'll have plenty of those this year," Ivy told the pups. "I'm planning a feast for all our friends!"

"There will be mashed potatoes, baked squash, cornbread stuffing, turkey with gravy, cranberry sauce, and apple and pumpkin pies for dessert!" Ivy said dreamily. "It will be just *perfect.*"

Montana put a bag of apples and a pumpkin in their cart. "Well, I really like grocery shopping, but I'm not much of a cook."

"Then you and Clarissa can help with the supplies," Ivy told her friend. "Everyone will have to pitch in to make the Thanksgiving feast perfect."

"Sure, Ivy," Clarissa barked. "We're happy to help."

"Great," Ivy replied. "I'll make a list of everything I'll need, and you and Montana can get it the week before Thanksgiving."

"No problem," Montana agreed.

"I'll also need some puppies to clean and decorate Puppyville Manor," Ivy said. "Someone will have to help me with the cooking, too."

"Wow, Ivy," Clarissa said with a frown. "That sounds like a lot of work."

Ivy nodded. "It is, but it will be worth it," she said. "It will be a perfect Thanksgiving!"

Back at Puppyville Manor, Ivy asked more friends to help with her feast. She put Spike and Sammy in charge of music. Then she saw Fuji and Freddy drawing.

"You two are good at crafts," Ivy told them. "You can be in charge of making decorations."

"We're going to be pretty busy designing this float for the Puppyville Thanksgiving Parade," Fuji said.

"But we can try to squeeze in a few decorations," Freddy added.

"And I'll need help with the cooking, Gigi," Ivy told her friend. "I am the chef, of course, but you can be my *sous chef*. That's French for 'assistant.'"

"*Oui*, Ivy, I will help you with the food," Gigi agreed with a toss of her head. "And I *do* know what a *sous chef* is. I am French, after all!"

Ivy waved a paw impatiently.

"I know, I know," she barked. "Sorry — there's just so much to do!"

And with that, she was out the door.

"Oh, my!" Gigi huffed. "Someone is being *very* bossy!"
Fuji nodded in agreement.

"I don't think she means to be," Freddy said gently. "She's just excited about Thanksgiving."

Ivy spent the next few days reading recipes and planning the perfect meal.

She even made handmade menus for everyone.

The day before Thanksgiving, Montana and Clarissa were on their way to yoga class when Ivy handed them a long list of ingredients for the feast.

"Do you think you can get the shopping done today?" Ivy asked her friends. "I'll need those supplies first thing tomorrow morning."

"We'll try, Ivy," Clarissa said. "But first we're going to yoga class."

"You should come with us," Montana added.

"Oh, I can't," Ivy said. "I have too much to do!"

Ivy decided to check on Sammy and Spike to find out what music they had chosen, but they were busy dancing.

"Have you two picked the songs for the Thanksgiving feast?" Ivy asked.

"Not yet," Sammy said with a shake of her head. "But we will."

Finally, Ivy checked in with Freddy and Fuji. They were busy putting the finishing touches on their parade float.

"Are the decorations for the feast done yet?" Ivy asked.

Fuji shook her head.

"Sorry, Ivy," Freddy said. "We haven't had a chance to start making the decorations. We've been busy working on this float."

Ivy was disappointed about the decorations, but she perked up when she saw Montana and Clarissa return with full shopping bags.

"Great!" Ivy said. "At least Gigi and I can start cooking."

"Well, we have some bad news," Montana said hesitantly. "The store was out of turkey and cranberries . . ."

"And squash and corn bread, too," Clarissa added, hanging her head. "I'm afraid we left the shopping until the last minute."

"Sorry," Montana said meekly. "But they did have apples and pumpkins, so we can still have pie."

Ivy was crushed. "Thanksgiving is ruined," she said with a sad sigh. "We can't celebrate without turkey and a big feast."

"Sure we can, Ivy," Fuji said. "Thanksgiving is about
giving thanks for what you have, and we've got a lot to
be thankful for. After all, we have each other."

She put her paw around Ivy's shoulder.

"Fuji's right!" Freddy agreed. "We can still have a really fun Thanksgiving. Fuji and I were going to ride on our float in the Puppyville Thanksgiving Parade. If we all work together, every puppy can wear a costume and join us."

"And afterward we can have a dessert feast with lots of pie!" Montana added.

Ivy smiled. "I guess that does sound like fun," she said. "Gigi and I can bake tonight while everyone else works on costumes."

"It's a plan!" Fuji barked.

That night, Gigi and Ivy baked pie after pie
after pie.

The other puppies made special costumes for the parade.

"All we need now is a sign for our float," Fuji said as she unrolled a banner and dug through her box of paints and brushes. "What should we put on it?"

"I know!" Sammy replied. She leaned over to whisper her idea in Fuji's ear.

"Perfect!" Fuji exclaimed.

"You're the best friends a puppy could ask for," Ivy told the others as she rode on the float. "Thanks for making this a perfect Thanksgiving!"

After the parade, everyone returned to Puppyville Manor for a dessert feast of apple and pumpkin pies.

Ivy bit into a piece of pie.
"What a sweet ending to the perfect day!"